P9-CEI-631

SADIQ
and the
Gamers

BY SIMAN NUURALI

ART BY CHRISTOS SKALTSAS

WITHDRAWN

BEAVERTON CITY LIBRARY
Beaverton, OR 97005
Member of Washington County
COOPERATIVE LIBRARY SERVICES
7717 5239

PICTURE WINDOW BOOKS
a capstone imprint

Published by Picture Window Books, an imprint of Capstone.
1710 Roe Crest Drive
North Mankato, Minnesota 56003
capstonepub.com

Copyright © 2022 by Capstone. All rights reserved. No part of this
publication may be reproduced in whole or in part, or stored in a
retrieval system, or transmitted in any form or by any means, electronic,
mechanical, photocopying, recording, or otherwise, without written
permission of the publisher.

Library of Congress Cataloging-in-Publication Data is available
on the Library of Congress website.
ISBN: 9781663909824 (hardcover)
ISBN: 9781663921918 (paperback)
ISBN: 9781663909794 (ebook pdf)

Summary: Sadiq and his friends are starting a video game club at school.
They have fun playing together and planning a tournament for the whole
school to participate in. But when their club needs a service project, the
club members are stumped. How can they help people with video games?
Then, during a visit to an assisted-living home called Harmony House,
Sadiq meets a man named Mr. Soto who could use some cheering up.
Could gaming be a way to help the residents at Harmony House?

Designer: Tracy Davies
Design Elements: Shutterstock/Irtsya

Printed and bound in the USA. 4270

TABLE OF CONTENTS

HI, I'M SADIQ! MY FAMILY AND I LIVE IN MINNESOTA, BUT MY PARENTS ARE FROM SOMALIA. SOMETIMES WE SPEAK SOMALI AT HOME.
I'D LIKE YOU TO MEET MY FAMILY AND LEARN SOME INTERESTING FACTS AND TERMS FROM OUR CULTURE.
Baba
Hooyo
Nuurali
Aliya
Rania
Amina

FACTS ABOUT SOMALIA

- Somali people come from many different clans.
- Many Somalis are nomadic. That means they travel from place to place. They search for water, food, and land for their animals.
- Somalia is mostly desert. It doesn't rain often there.
- The camel is an important animal to Somali people. Camels can survive a long time without food or water.
- Around ninety-nine percent of all Somalis are Muslim.

SOMALI TERMS

baba (BAH-baah)—a common word for father

hooyo (HOY-yoh)—mother

qalbi (KUHL-bee)—my heart

salaam (sa-LAHM)—a short form of Arabic greeting, used by many Muslims. It also means "peace."

wiilkeyga (wil-KAY-gaah)—my son

CHAPTER 1

THE GAMERS MEET

At the end of school on Friday, Sadiq, Manny, and Zuza walked to the school library. It was time for the first meeting of the Gamers, their new video game club!

When the boys got to the library, Mr. Kim was setting up a table. He was the club advisor.

"Hi, Mr. Kim!" Sadiq called out.

"Hello!" Mr. Kim said. "Would you please get some chairs for us? Arrange them around this table so we can all see each other."

The boys collected chairs and arranged them. Several other students arrived and started helping. Soon the meeting began. They had a lot to talk about as they planned how the club would work.

"How often should we meet?" asked Halah. She was in Sadiq's class.

"Maybe once a month?" said another student named Nimo.

"I don't think that's enough," said Sadiq. "It might be better if we meet once a week."

"That way we can talk about new games," said Zaza.

"Have you all thought about what you want the club to do?" asked Mr. Kim.

"Yes!" replied Sadiq. "Manny, Zaza, and I had an idea to hold a tournament."

"That's a great idea!" said Mr. Kim. The students around the table all nodded at this idea. "What kind of tournament are you thinking of?"

"A few of us really like *Screech Master 7000*," said Safwan.

"Is that the racing game?" asked Nimo. "My brother really likes that one!"

"I think lots of people like it," said Sadiq. "We could invite students to compete."

"Should we have prizes?" asked Halah, smiling. "I'm really good at it and could win."

"What do you guys think?" asked Sadiq. "We can award prizes to the fastest players at the end."

"What sort of prizes?" asked Nimo. "We would have to pay for them."

"What if we sell tickets to enter the tournament?" asked Zaza. "Then we can buy prizes with the ticket money."

"These are all great ideas to think about," said Mr. Kim. "Now let's discuss the topic of your service pledge."

"What is that?" asked Manny.

"Remember how you helped people when you were in other clubs?" said Mr. Kim. "It's the same thing. A club should find a way to help others."

"We hadn't thought about that," replied Manny. "What can we do for a service pledge with video games?"

The club members were quiet as they thought about what to do.

"We could teach younger kids how to play," Nimo suggested.

"I don't think we can do that," said Halah. "My mom doesn't let my younger brother play video games. She says he's too young."

"Same here," said Safwan. "My mom doesn't let my sister Salma play with me."

"Does anyone else have an idea?" asked Sadiq, looking around.

"Should we think about it? We can come back with ideas next week," said Zaza.

"Would that be okay, Mr. Kim?" asked Sadiq. "We can plan it for our next meeting."

"That would be fine," replied Mr. Kim, smiling. "It's enough time for you all to come up with some great ideas!"

The students spent the next few minutes putting the chairs back and straightening up. They didn't want the librarian to find it untidy!

CHAPTER 2

SADIQ VOLUNTEERS

Saturday morning was sunny and warm. Sadiq was eating breakfast with his family.

"Are you still coming with me, Sadiq?" asked *Hooyo*. "We will have to leave soon for Harmony House."

"Yes, Hooyo!" replied Sadiq. "I am almost done eating. I just have to grab my backpack."

Hooyo volunteered at an assisted-living home a couple days a week. Sadiq loved to go with her to help out.

"Do you want to practice *Screech* tonight?" asked Nuurali. "I could show you those tricks I told you about."

"Yes, Nuurali!" replied Sadiq. "That would be great. Zaza beat me last time we played."

"Hurry up before Hooyo leaves you," said Nuurali, teasing. He gently elbowed his younger brother as he got up from the table.

Sadiq finished his breakfast and put his dishes in the sink. He knew Hooyo didn't like to be kept waiting.

"Coming!" he shouted.

***

When they arrived at Harmony House, Hooyo went to check in at the main office.

"You can go in the game room, *qalbi*," she said. "I just have to sign us in, then I'll join you."

Sadiq walked to the game room, greeting residents on the way. They all knew him, and most smiled at him.

"Hi, Mr. Wesman!" Sadiq called out.

"Hi there, Sadiq!" replied Mr. Wesman. "Up for a game of checkers today?"

"Okay! I think I might finally beat you," replied Sadiq, laughing.

"Ha!" said Mr. Wesman. "I look forward to it. The board is all set up. Let's begin after I finish reading the paper."

Magazines and newspapers were scattered on a nearby table. Sadiq tidied them up. As Sadiq put some books back on the shelf, he noticed an older man sitting alone. Sadiq had never seen him before. He looked sad and lonely by himself in the corner.

"Hi there!" said Sadiq, walking up. "My name is Sadiq Mohamed. I work here sometimes with my mom."

"Hello, young man," replied the man softly. "My name is Mr. Soto."

"It's very nice to meet you," said Sadiq.

"Nice to meet you too," replied Mr. Soto. But instead of looking at Sadiq, he stared out the window. He had a race car magazine on his lap.

"Do you need anything?" asked Sadiq. "I could get you books if you like."

"No, thanks," replied Mr. Soto. He kept looking out the window.

Sadiq decided Mr. Soto wanted to be left alone.

"Well, let me know if there's anything I can do," Sadiq said to him.

As he walked away, he saw three residents at another table. They were playing cards and laughing. They looked like they were having fun. Sadiq wished Mr. Soto could have fun too.

CHAPTER 3

PRACTICING FOR THE TOURNAMENT

Later that day, Sadiq and his family ate dinner together at home.

"Did you have fun with your hooyo at Harmony House?" asked *Baba*.

"Yes, Baba," replied Sadiq, smiling. "I played checkers with Mr. Wesman. He always wins."

"That's great, qalbi," said Baba. "What else did you do?"

"I helped Hooyo wash dishes," replied Sadiq. "I also met a new resident. His name is Mr. Soto."

"What was he like?" asked Nuurali.

"I don't really know," said Sadiq. "He was nice but didn't say a whole lot. He seemed sad."

"Oh, that's too bad," said his sister Aliya.

"Hooyo, do you know why Mr. Soto was sad?" asked Sadiq.

"I know he moved in just last month," replied Hooyo. "It was soon after his wife died. He doesn't talk a lot. He keeps to himself."

"Oh," said Sadiq, looking down. "I wonder if we can cheer him up."

"Maybe once he settles in properly he'll open up," said Baba.

After dinner, everyone helped clear the table.

"Hey, Sadiq," Nuurali said when they were done. "Do you still want to play *Screech*? I have time to play for a little bit."

"Race you!" called Sadiq, running up the stairs.

"I'll get you next time!" said Nuurali, coming after him.

Sadiq turned on the computer while Nuurali got out the headsets.

"Thanks for helping me, Nuurali," said Sadiq. "I can't get past level eleven, and I don't know why."

"Why don't you show me," said Nuurali. "Are you getting stuck on that 200 marker? A lot of people spin out in that slippery turn."

"That's it!" said Sadiq. "How did you know? It happens every single time."

"I spent three weeks stuck at that level," said Nuurali, laughing. "I finally figured it out."

"Do you lose points if you slow down there?" asked Sadiq. "I kept my speed so I wouldn't lose points. But then I would always spin out."

"You do lose points," replied Nuurali. "But you can make them up once you come out of the turn."

The boys put on their headsets.

Sadiq started the game where he had left off, at level eleven. Soon he was approaching the tricky part.

"Keep that speed for now," said Nuurali. "Here comes the 175 marker, so move one lane to the left."

"Okay, done! Now what?" asked Sadiq. He kept his eyes on the screen.

"There's the 200 marker," said Nuurali. "Press the down arrow and drop your speed to about fifty. Now, take the corner."

"Like this?" asked Sadiq. His tires screeched, but just a little.

"Just like that," replied Nuurali. "It's okay to slide a little like that."

Sadiq nodded.

"Okay, you're coming out now.
Increase your speed slowly," Nuurali said.

"Nuurali! I am doing it!" shouted
Sadiq, excited. "I am not spinning out!"

"Yes, I can see, Sadiq," said Nuurali, laughing. "But concentrate! You could still lose control."

"This is so great!" shouted Sadiq. "I can't believe it!"

"Straighten out," said Nuurali. "Good! And you're on your way to level twelve."

"I did it!" shouted Sadiq.

The two brothers played *Screech* for an hour. Then it was time to brush their teeth and go to bed.

"Good night, Nuurali," said Sadiq once they were in bed. He turned over to recite his prayers.

"Good night, Sadiq," said Nuurali.

They lay in the dark for a few minutes. Then Sadiq remembered something.

"Oh, no!" he said, sitting up. He had forgotten all about the service pledge.

"What's wrong?" asked Nuurali.

"I just forgot something I had to do," replied Sadiq. "I'll do it tomorrow."

That night Sadiq had a dream. He was a race car driver in *Screech Master 7000*! He was trying to pass the lead car on his way to winning. Just as he passed the car, Sadiq looked over. The driver in the lead car was Mr. Soto!

CHAPTER 4

SADIQ VISITS MR. SOTO

Next Friday after school, Sadiq and his friends went to the library for the Gamers meeting. Mr. Kim had art supplies laid out on the tables. There were markers, paints, glitter, and poster board. Once everyone was there, they all began to work on posters. They wanted to advertise their tournament so lots of kids would sign up.

"We still haven't picked a service pledge," said Nimo, coloring a picture of a game controller. "Maybe we could donate the money from the ticket sales."

"I don't think that's fair," said Halah. "Lots of kids are using their own allowance to buy a ticket to the tournament. They expect a chance to win prizes."

Sadiq thought about Mr. Soto. He looked so sad and lonely. Sadiq wanted to help him, but he didn't know how.

"Why don't you go put up posters," said Mr. Kim. "You can take one more week to decide on the service pledge."

***

Hooyo was putting on her shoes when Sadiq came downstairs.

"*Salaam*, Hooyo," said Sadiq. "Are you going somewhere?"

"Yes, qalbi," replied Hooyo, smiling. "I am going to volunteer at Harmony House."

"Oh, right!" said Sadiq. "It's Saturday! Can I come with you? I could do my homework there."

"Of course!" replied Hooyo. "Good thing you have your shoes and backpack."

She winked at him and smiled. Sadiq could never find his shoes when it was time to go. His family liked to tease him about it.

When they arrived at Harmony House, Sadiq made his way to the game room. He found Mr. Soto sitting quietly by the window.

"Hi, Mr. Soto," said Sadiq as he waved.

Mr. Soto waved back but didn't say anything.

Sadiq sat down at an empty table. He took out his books and started on his homework. He finished quickly, then pulled out his tablet to play *Screech*. He wanted to practice as much as he could.

"Downshift to second gear on that curve. You'll get more traction that way."

Sadiq looked up, startled. He had been concentrating on the game. He hadn't noticed Mr. Soto standing by his shoulder.

"You know *Screech*?" asked Sadiq. His eyes were wide in surprise.

Sadiq took Mr. Soto's advice, and it helped. He finished the race with his best time ever!

"How did you know to do that?" asked Sadiq.

"I used to race cars when I was younger," Mr. Soto replied. "I haven't done it for many years now. But I still remember some of the tricks."

Mr. Soto smiled at Sadiq.

"That's awesome! Thanks!" said Sadiq. He couldn't wait to tell Nuurali.

Sadiq suddenly had an idea. His eyes lit up as he turned to Mr. Soto.

"Mr. Soto," said Sadiq, "would you like to join our video game club?"

Mr. Soto shook his head. "I've never played before. I don't think I could."

"Don't worry, Mr. Soto," said Sadiq. "We can show you."

"Well," said Mr. Soto, "sure, why not?"

When Sadiq left Harmony House that day, he was excited. He couldn't wait for the Gamers to meet Mr. Soto and the other residents.

CHAPTER 5

HARMONY HOUSE

"Mr. Soto is really great," said Sadiq. "All the residents are. I can't wait for you guys to meet them!"

Mr. Kim was driving Sadiq and the rest of the club to Harmony House. Sadiq had talked the members into having their meeting there.

Mr. Kim pulled into the parking lot and found a place to park.

"Okay, kids, remember your manners," he said as he turned off the van. Everyone piled out and made their way inside.

The kids waited while Mr. Kim checked them in at the office. Some of them were nervous.

"It's okay, you guys," said Sadiq. "Everyone here is really friendly!"

Sadiq led Mr. Kim and the kids to Mr. Soto's table in the game room.

"Hi, Mr. Soto!" said Sadiq. "These are my friends in the video game club. Remember the ones I told you about?"

"Oh, yes," replied Mr. Soto.

"Everyone, meet Mr. Soto!" said Sadiq.

Sadiq was grinning from ear to ear. "I told my friends how you helped me, Mr. Soto. They wanted to meet you!"

"Well, I didn't do much," said Mr. Soto with a shrug. "I only gave him one tip."

"Are you ready to play a game?" asked Sadiq.

"Ready," said Mr. Soto. "Maybe I can learn from *you* this time."

Sadiq smiled and took out his tablet. The other kids reached into their bags and took out theirs too. They all sat around Mr. Soto's table.

"Do you want to start with *Screech*?" asked Halah. "I heard you like racing."

"It does look cool," said Mr. Soto, "but I've never played a video game before."

"You're really going to like it!" said Sadiq. "You can use my tablet."

He handed his tablet to Mr. Soto. The kids crowded around them. Sadiq showed Mr. Soto how to start the game and what to push to control the race car.

Soon the kids were cheering on Mr. Soto.

"Okay, everyone settle down," said Mr. Kim. "Remember, we can't be *too* loud."

The kids lowered their voices. They whispered excitedly as they showed Mr. Soto how to play.

"Watch out, Mr. Soto," said Zaza. "You have to be careful on that turn!"

Crash!

"Oh no!" said Mr. Soto with a laugh. "I've spun out! I wasn't as careful as I should have been, Zaza."

"That's okay, Mr. Soto," said Manny. "That's always a tough turn in that level."

"This is the most fun I have had in ages!" said Mr. Soto. He was smiling and clapped his hands.

"Us too!" said Sadiq.

Other residents came to see what the noise was about. When they saw Mr. Soto laughing with the kids, many of them wanted to play too!

Soon it was time to go. "Say goodbye to your new friends," said Mr. Kim to his students. "Make sure to thank them!"

"Goodbye!" called out the kids. "Thanks for gaming with us!"

The Gamers walked to Mr. Kim's van.

"The residents had a really great time with you," said Mr. Kim. "Maybe visiting Harmony House could be your service pledge."

"Great idea!" said Halah.

Everyone agreed. Their service pledge was going to be fun!

CHAPTER 6

THE GAMERS COMPETE!

After that, the Gamers held their weekly meetings at Harmony House. They made new friends. One of them was Mr. Henry. He used to be a builder before he retired. The kids showed him a game called *Stack Builder*.

"You have to build a whole house before the timer runs out!" said Halah. "It's really hard to do."

"Let's give it a shot!" said Mr. Henry.

Halah handed Mr. Henry her tablet. She started a new game and showed him what to do. Soon she was cheering on Mr. Henry. He was about to beat the clock!

"There's one minute left, Mr. Henry," squealed Halah. "You still have to put the two windows in!"

"And . . . done!" said Mr. Henry, raising his hand in victory. "With three seconds left!"

"Great job, Mr. Henry!" cheered Halah.

The kids also met Ms. Filson, a resident who used to be a chemist. The kids showed Ms. Filson a science game.

In the game, players worked in a lab and did experiments. But they had to do it without blowing things up!

Sadiq looked forward to the Gamers meeting at Harmony House every week. At each meeting, the residents played video games with the students. The kids taught the residents gaming tricks, and the residents taught the gamers some things too!

Even better, they had made friends with the residents of Harmony House.

***

The next month was the *Screech* tournament. It was a Friday evening. There were six teams. Each team sat at a table together in the gym.

Sadiq, Manny, Zaza, and Halah were competing for the club. They had spent a lot of time practicing and felt ready for the tournament.

"Do you think we'll win?" asked Zaza. He was nervous and bouncing on the balls of his feet.

"I hope so," said Sadiq. "Let's try our best and just have fun!"

Mr. Kim stepped up to the microphone. Everyone became quiet.

"The rules are as follows," he said. "Do not touch your tablets until I start the clock. You have to put your tablets down when the clock stops. The team with the highest average score wins."

Mr. Kim looked out at all the kids.
"Ready. Set. Go!" he said and started
the clock.

Everyone picked up their tablet and
launched the game. The *Screech Master
7000* tournament was on!

There was a lot of cheering in
the gym from students and families
Everyone wanted their team to win!

Sadiq focused on his game. He tried
to remember the driving tricks Mr. Soto
taught him. Before he knew it, the
timer went off.

"And that's time!" called Mr. Kim.
"The clock has stopped. Please set down
your tablets."

Mr. Kim went around to each table.
He checked the score on each tablet.

Soon Mr. Kim returned to the front of the gym.

"Okay, I have the tournament results," Mr. Kim said into the microphone. "In first place, we have the Gamers Club! Great job!"

The Gamers cheered and ran to the stage. They were very excited, and they proudly accepted their trophy.

***

The next day, Sadiq and the rest of the Gamers went back to Harmony House for a special visit. Hooyo had agreed to drive them to see Mr. Soto.

"We won the tournament, Mr. Soto!" said Sadiq, smiling.

"Congratulations!" said Mr. Soto. He gave them all high fives.

"We talked, and we want you to have the trophy," Sadiq said. "Your tricks helped us win it!"

"Thank you very much, Sadiq," said Mr. Soto. "I am very proud of you all. I love the trophy and will keep it next to my bed."

"Would you like to play a game now, Mr. Soto?" asked Sadiq.

"Oh yes!" said Mr. Soto, smiling. "This time, I might even beat you."

GLOSSARY

assisted living (uh-SIS-ted LIV-ing)—a place to live for older people who need help with daily tasks

chemist (KEH-mist)—a person who is trained in the scientific study of substances, what they are made of, and how they react with each other

compete (kum-PEET)—to participate and try to win in a game or competition

experiment (ek-SPEH-ruh-ment)—a test that is used to find out something

microphone (MYK-ruh-fone)—an electronic device that is used to make a sound, such as a voice, louder

pledge (PLEJ)—a promise to do something

resident (REZ-uh-dent)—a person who lives or stays somewhere

service (SUR-viss)—an act of useful help given to someone who needs it

spin out (SPIN OWT)—to lose control of a vehicle and spin in a circle

tablet (TAB-lit)—a small, flat, portable computer

tournament (TUR-nuh-ment)—a contest in which people can compete at different games to win

traction (TRAK-shun)—the friction or gripping power that keeps a moving body from slipping on a surface

trophy (TROH-fee)—a prize or award such as a cup, small statue, or plaque given to winners in a competition

volunteer (VOL-uhn-TEER)—a person who agrees to do something helpful on their own time and without being paid

TALK ABOUT IT

1. Hooyo told Sadiq that Mr. Soto's wife died recently, and that he was often sad and quiet. How do you think Mr. Soto felt about the kids coming to play with him?

2. Mr. Kim told the Gamers they needed to choose a service pledge for their club. Why is this important? Can you think of other service pledges you could do with your friends?

3. Sadiq won the tournament, but he didn't do it alone. Who else helped him play so well? How did each of these people help him?

WRITE IT DOWN

1. Imagine a popular video game company has asked you to invent a video game. What kind of game would it be? What would the rules be? Draw a picture of it and write down how the game is played.

2. Have you ever felt sad or lonely or known someone who felt that way? What made you or that person feel better? Write about what happened.

3. Write a paragraph about a service pledge or project you have done. What was the project or pledge, and why did you choose it? How did it feel to volunteer? If you have never done a service project, write about one you would like to try.

WRITE A LETTER TO SOMEONE IN AN ASSISTED-LIVING HOME

When Sadiq went to Harmony House, he connected with someone who really needed a friend. If you can't volunteer in person, you can make friends with a resident (or many residents!) in an assisted-living home by writing them a letter. Your letter just might cheer up someone who needs it!

WHAT YOU NEED:

pencil or pen and paper
(or a computer and printer)
envelope
stamp

WHAT TO DO:

1. Ask an adult to help you find an assisted-living home that will accept letters. You might know someone who lives there, or you might write a letter for all the residents to read.

2. Gather your supplies and make sure you have a dry, clean surface like a desk to write on. If you're using a computer or tablet, turn on a word processing program.

3. Start your letter with "Dear Coco," filling in the blank with the person's name or with something like "residents of meow."

4. Some topics you can write about in your letter include the weather, what you have been up to at school, or even some of your favorite foods. You can also tell a joke or draw a picture.

5. Ask the residents some questions about themselves. You can ask about their hobbies, books they are reading, or shows they watch. Ask about their friends or family members. You can ask them to share a joke of their own! Be sure to encourage them to write back with their answers.

6. Sign your name at the end.

7. Print your letter if you wrote it on a computer and sign your name. Fold it, place it in an envelope, and seal it.

8. Have an adult help you address it and put a stamp on the envelope. Then drop your letter in the mail. The resident will receive it in a few days!

In some cases, sending an email may be easier, but receiving an actual letter in the mail can feel more special. If the resident writes back to you, you will find out for yourself!

CREATORS

Siman Nuurali grew up in Kenya. She now lives in Minnesota. Siman and her family are Somali—just like Sadiq and his family! She and her five children love to play badminton and board games together. Siman works at Children's Hospital and in her free time she enjoys writing and reading.

Christos Skaltsas was born and raised in Athens, Greece. For the past fifteen years, he has worked as a freelance illustrator for children's book publishers. In his free time, he loves playing with his son, collecting vinyl records, and traveling around the world.